It's Not a Dinosaur!

Stacy McAnulty
illustrations by Mike Boldt

A STEPPING STONE BOOK™
Random House New York

Text copyright © 2016 by Stacy McAnulty
Cover art and interior illustrations copyright © 2016 by Mike Boldt

All rights reserved. Published in the United States by Random House Children's Books, a division of Penguin Random House LLC, New York.

Random House and the colophon are registered trademarks and A Stepping Stone Book and the colophon are trademarks of Penguin Random House LLC.

Visit us on the Web!
SteppingStonesBooks.com
randomhousekids.com

Educators and librarians, for a variety of teaching tools,
visit us at RHTeachersLibrarians.com

Library of Congress Cataloging-in-Publication Data
Names: McAnulty, Stacy, author. | Boldt, Mike, illustrator.
Title: It's not a dinosaur! / by Stacy McAnulty ; illustrated by Mike Boldt.
Other titles: It is not a dinosaur
Description: New York : Random House, [2016] | Series: Dino files ; #3 |
Summary: When photographs of Peanut the dinosaur appear on the Web,
Frank's father arrives in Wyoming with a story about the prehistoric reptile he
saw nearby twenty years earlier.
Identifiers: LCCN 2015037986 | ISBN 978-0-553-52197-9 (hardback) |
ISBN 978-0-553-52198-6 (hardcover library binding) |
ISBN 978-0-553-52199-3 (ebook)
Subjects: | CYAC: Prehistoric animals—Fiction. | Dinosaurs—Fiction. | Animals—
Infancy—Fiction. | Cousins—Fiction. | Paleontology—Fiction.
BISAC: JUVENILE FICTION / Animals / Dinosaurs & Prehistoric Creatures. |
JUVENILE FICTION / Action & Adventure / General. | JUVENILE FICTION /
Humorous Stories.
Classification: LCC PZ7.M47825255 Its 2016 | DDC [Fic]—dc23

Printed in the United States of America
10 9 8 7 6 5 4 3 2 1

This book has been officially leveled by using
the F&P Text Level Gradient™ Leveling System.

Random House Children's Books supports the First Amendment
and celebrates the right to read.

For my McParents, Bob and Fran

CONTENTS

Dear Reader,

Can I trust you? Because I only share my stories with kids I trust. It may seem like a lot of people know my secrets. But there are many, many more who don't. So I need you to take an oath. Hold up your right hand and say:

I, (now say your name), promise to keep this amazing story locked in my brain forever. I won't say anything to anyone, even if I'm tickle-tortured. If I do spill Frank Mudd's secrets, may I grow gills on my forehead and webbed toes.

Thank you. You can start reading now.

Sincerely,
Frank Mudd
Future Paleontologist*

*All the dinosaur words can be found in my glossary.

Not Very Popular

If **I were** president, I would make this a law. *You're not allowed to take pictures of someone's dinosaur without asking.*

Two days ago, a camera repair guy took pictures of my baby dinosaur. He put them on the Internet. I've been trying to keep Peanut a secret for weeks. Now that's over.

"What are we going to do?" I ask Gram. And not for the first time.

"Frank, relax," she says. Also, not for the first time.

"Only one thousand people have seen the pictures," my cousin Samantha says. "You're not an Internet star until you have a million views."

Sam picks up Peanut and kisses his horn. "Sorry, buddy. You're not very popular."

"Not yet!" I yell. "The pictures have only been up for two days."

"Maybe this will all just settle down," PopPop says. "No need to get upset."

I let out a loud puff of air. No one is taking this seriously. Except the Starks. Mr. and Mrs. Stark, their daughter, and their *Velociraptor* were staying with us. My grandparents' house used to be a safe place for secret dinosaurs and people who love them. But the Starks packed up their RV and left yesterday. That's what Peanut and I should be doing.

"Frank, Peanut will be fine," Gram says. "He may no longer be a secret, but he is still safe here at DECoW."

My grandparents own the Dinosaur Education Center of Wyoming. We call it DECoW. It's the perfect place to raise a dinosaur. They have lots of land, and so do their neighbors. This is a good thing because Peanut is going to be huge. We know this because of fossils we found. Someday he will make elephants look small.

I believe Gram. But just in case, I go to my room and pack a bag for me, Peanut, and my cat, Saurus. I'm ready if we need to make a quick getaway.

The next morning, DECoW is the same old DECoW. Only seven cars are parked in the lot near the museum where we keep all the fossils.

I was worried that there would be a million.

I stand by the living room window, watching.

"Frank, eat," Gram says. She has made waffles for Sam and me. Peanut gets a leaf mixture. We call it Peanut salad. Saurus gets a can of cat food.

"Can I have his waffles?" Sam asks.

"No," I say, because Gram makes the best waffles.

"I want you kids to stay close to the house today," Gram says. "And keep Peanut inside."

"Why?" I ask. My stomach gets nervous and squishy.

"No reason," Gram answers. I don't believe her.

"Peanut's pictures have over ten thousand likes," Sam says. Then she shoves another huge piece of waffle in her mouth.

"That's it. I'm leaving." I drop my fork and grab my dinosaur. "Can you make me a sandwich for the road?"

"Frank, please." Gram shakes her head. "We will figure this out."

"It's not like someone is going to take him away from us," Sam says. "Right?"

"Of course not." Gram turns to a sink full of dishes. "No one is going to come to the door and take our dinosaur."

Just then, there's a knock on the front door.

I Know That Voice

"**H**ide!" **I scream.** Peanut and I dive under the kitchen table.

The door slowly opens before Gram can get to it. I shake in my slippers.

"Hello," a voice calls out. "Anyone home?"

I know that voice.

"Dad!" I crawl out from under the table.

My dad stands in the living room. I run into

his arms, and he hugs me tight. He smells like the green soap we use at home.

"What are you doing here?" I ask. Mom, Dad, Saurus, and I live in North Carolina. That's where I go to school. I just spend the summers in Wyoming. North Carolina is at least two long plane rides away.

"I'm here about a dinosaur." Dad holds a blurry picture of Peanut. "Anyone want to explain?"

"I will," Sam says. "Have a seat, Uncle Brian. This is a long story." She pulls her plastic microphone from her pocket. She carries it everywhere. She also talks to an invisible TV camera a lot. She thinks she'll be famous someday.

Peanut wanders into the living room. He

brushes against Dad's leg. Then he jumps into an empty chair near the window.

"Was that . . . ?" Dad can't finish his thought.

"Yes." Gram gives him a hug. "Sam is right. You're going to want to sit."

Dad plops down on the couch. Saurus leaps onto his lap, and Dad scratches her chin. Saurus purrs like a motor.

"So here's the story." Sam explains how Gram found the egg fossil a few weeks ago. And how Saurus and I sat on it. And how Peanut hatched. And how Sam and I tried to keep him a secret.

And how Aaron from next door dino-napped Peanut. And how Peanut got sick on cookies and candy and had to go to the vet.

"Wow," Dad says. "You should write a book about all of this."

I smile and say, "I am."

"We're going to build Peanut a home," Sam says. "A big one. The Crabtrees from next door are going to help too."

"Why didn't you tell your mom and me about Peanut?" Dad asks.

"I didn't want to tell you over the phone," I say. "He *was* a secret."

"And spies could be listening to our phone calls," Sam says. Her eyes grow really big.

I planned to tell Mom and Dad when they came to pick me up at the end of summer. Dad is just a lot early. I haven't even had enough time to work on my begging. *Can I please, please, please live at DECoW with Peanut?*

"How did you hear about Peanut?" Gram asks.

"A friend of mine emailed me the picture. I got on the next plane." Dad hands me Saurus. "I had to see with my own eyes."

Dad tiptoes toward Peanut, who is sleeping on the chair. He bends down to get a closer look.

"What is he?" Dad pushes his glasses up.

"Nothing we've ever seen," Gram says. "The kids call him a *Wyomingasaurus*."

My dad is a paleontologist too. He works at a college and teaches classes about prehistoric plants.

"Fascinating." Dad's nose is almost touching Peanut's horn.

Suddenly, Peanut wakes up. He jumps and crashes into Dad's face. Dad's glasses fall to the floor.

"Ow." Dad rubs his nose.

"Are you okay?" I ask.

"Is Peanut okay?" Sam asks.

Peanut runs out of the room and up the stairs.

"I'm fine," Dad says. "That little dinosaur is fast. I hope you keep a good eye on him."

"We try," Sam says.

For dinner, PopPop grills chicken. Peanut doesn't have any because he's an herbivore. He eats a whole head of cabbage and a bag of carrots.

"He has a good appetite," Dad says. "How big is he?"

"Eighteen pounds," I say. "He's doubled his weight from when he hatched." Gram measures him every morning. We keep track of what he eats, his size, and other important stuff. It's what good scientists do.

"I used to dream of having my own dinosaur when I was a boy," Dad says.

PopPop laughs. "It's all you ever asked for. Every birthday. Every holiday."

Dad looks down at his plate and shakes his head. "But you always said no."

PopPop and Gram glance at each other super quick. Sam wrinkles her forehead. She's confused like me.

"That's because dinosaurs are extinct," Sam says. "Or at least we thought they were."

"Yes," Gram says. "And we let you have that snake. What was his name?"

"Teddy Rex," Dad mumbles. "But a snake is not the same as a dinosaur."

I give Dad a hug. "Not the same at all."

An Eel with Four Legs

A shaking wakes me up in the middle of the night. At first I think it's Peanut jumping on the bed. He does that sometimes.

"Frank, wake up." It's my dad. He's shaking me by the shoulders.

"I'm awake. I'm awake. What's wrong?" I ask. My pets are awake too. Peanut stands on me. Saurus stretches by my feet.

"I need to tell you something." Dad sits on the edge of my bed. It's getting very crowded.

"What?"

"Or maybe I'll show you." Dad goes to the desk. It used to be his when he was a boy. The whole room used to be his. He pulls out the top drawer and flips it over. Pens and pencils fall to the floor. Peanut jumps up to see if there is anything good to eat.

A piece of paper is taped to the bottom of the drawer.

"Here." He unfolds it and hands it to me.

On the paper is a drawing. It looks like an eel but with four small legs. Written in the bottom corner is Dad's real name (Brian) and one word.

"*Nothosaurus,*" I read.

"Yes!" Dad says. "That's the creature I found when I was a boy." He taps the paper.

"Really?" I ask.

"No way," Sam says. She walks into my room without knocking and takes the picture. "Is this the dinosaur you always wanted, Uncle Brian?"

"It's not a dinosaur," I say. "The *Nothosaurus* is a prehistoric reptile that lived in water."

Sam rolls her eyes. "Aren't dinosaurs prehistoric reptiles?"

"Yes, but not all prehistoric reptiles are dinosaurs," I say. "Just like cats are mammals. But that doesn't mean all mammals are cats. You're a mammal, and you're not a cat."

"It's basically a dinosaur," Sam shoots back. I need to start a dinosaur school for her and other confused people.

"Do you want to hear my story?" Dad asks.

"Yes!" Sam and I both answer. We sit on my bed. Peanut curls up in her lap and Saurus in mine.

"I was twelve," Dad starts. "And I was canoe-ing on the river with three boys from Scouts. We stopped to take a bathroom break."

"There are rest stops on the river?" Sam asks.

"Boys don't need an actual bathroom," I answer.

"Gross." She sticks out her tongue.

"I finished my business and got back first," Dad continues. "And there it was. A *Nothosaurus*. Sunning itself right next to our canoe."

"Did it attack you?" Sam asks.

"No. It just stared at me. The Notho was longer than our boat. It had purple-gray skin. No scales. And large black eyes." Dad scratches his beard. "What a sight. It wasn't afraid at all. At least not until the other boys came out of the woods. They were laughing and joking and being pretty loud."

"Did the *Nothosaurus* attack them?" Sam asks excitedly.

"No, Sam. It dove back into the river before

the boys got a good look. One of them—a kid named Bart Matthews—saw part of the tail. He started screaming that it was a river monster. I tried to explain that it was a *Nothosaurus.* He didn't believe me. No one did."

"Not even Gram and PopPop?" I ask.

"I told them about it when I got home. They wanted to believe me," Dad says. "We went back to the river dozens of times. I never saw it again. As I grew older, I worried that I imagined the Notho."

"You didn't imagine it, Uncle Brian. If Peanut is real, I bet your river dinosaur is real too," Sam says.

"That's what I was thinking." Dad smiles.

"What about Bart Matthews?" I ask. "Did people believe him?"

"Bart always claimed it was a river monster. He drew a two-headed beast and told everyone in school that's what we found. So I drew my own picture. I didn't want to forget." Dad takes his paper back.

"Wait!" A thought hits my brain. "Is Bart the guy from the TV? Bart's River Monster Tours?"

"I've seen his commercials!" Sam yells. "My mom says he's crazy."

"That's him," Dad says.

"He's a friend of yours?" I ask.

"We aren't exactly friends," Dad explains. "I haven't seen the guy in twenty years. But tomorrow I think we should visit him."

Not in the Backyard

Dad has perfect timing. When the sun comes up, a news van comes with it. Pop-Pop talks to the reporters. They've come to see the dinosaur from the Internet. It won't be long before the whole world is at DECoW.

"I'll get the tent out of the garage," Gram says. "Frank, can you get three sleeping bags?"

"Wait, we're camping?" I ask.

"You love camping," Dad says.

"I like camping in the backyard," I correct him. In the backyard, you can still go inside for a snack or to use the toilet.

"It'll be great," Dad says. "I used to do this all the time as a kid."

"In the backyard," PopPop adds.

"Don't worry, boys." Sam stuffs a backpack full of gear. "I auditioned once for a TV show that takes place in the woods of California."

"Did you get the part?" I ask.

"No, but I did practice a lot," she says.

"Where?" I ask.

She shrugs. "In the backyard."

We each get a backpack. Gram gives us supplies like rope and a pot. PopPop fills a bag with food and water bottles.

"We also need this stuff," Dad says. He has a list longer than Peanut.

"How long are we going for?" I ask.

"Two months," Sam says. "Then we don't have to go back to school!"

"Just three days," Gram says. "That should be enough time for PopPop and me to get things settled here."

"And that will give us time to find the *Nothosaurus*," Dad says.

"Brian," PopPop says, "we always believed you saw something in the river. But I'll admit, I never thought it was a *Nothosaurus*. Not until I met Peanut. We should have tried harder to help you find it."

"We'll find the Notho now," Dad says. "Right, kids? Are we ready?"

"I want to use the indoor bathroom one more time," Sam says.

"Me too," I add.

Aaron Crabtree waits for us outside. He lives next door and helps us take care of Peanut sometimes. He doesn't have any gear.

"Aren't you coming?" I ask. Sam called him this morning to tell him about our trip.

"I can't. I've got the junior fishing tournament. I've won it three years in a row. I have to defend my crown," Aaron says.

"Do you really get a crown?" Sam asks.

"No, a trophy." Aaron picks up Peanut and hugs him. "I just wanted to say goodbye. And good luck."

"Thanks," I say.

"You know, there are rattlesnakes out there." He points to the path we'll be taking.

"And scorpions. And poisonous lizards."

"I know," Dad says with a shaky voice.

"That's enough, Aaron," Gram says. "They'll be fine."

Aaron pulls a small notebook out of his back pocket. It says: *All the Things That Can Kill You in Wyoming* by Aaron Crabtree.

"Just in case," he says.

Sam takes the notebook. "Cool."

"You better go before more news crews arrive," PopPop says. "I shut the gate, but they might ignore the Closed sign."

I put a leash on Peanut. Dad, Sam, and I say goodbye. We hug Gram and PopPop. Saurus sits on the front porch.

"Are you coming with us or not?" I ask. "You have to walk all on your own." Usually, Saurus is lazy and only travels in her catmobile. It's actually just an old stroller.

Saurus meows. I think that means no.

"Let's get going," Dad says. "We'll see you in three days."

Sam and I follow Dad. I think I have a blister already. Saurus stays on the porch.

"Why aren't we taking the truck?" I ask again.

"Spies might follow it," Sam says.

"They could also follow us walking," I say.

"There's a path that leads right to the river," Dad says. "It's just a few miles and all on DECoW property. I don't think there's much of a chance of our being followed."

"Dad, if you'd found the *Nothosaurus* again, do you think you would have kept him?" I ask.

"I don't know," Dad answers. "He was too big to fit in our bathtub."

"But maybe Gram and PopPop could have built him a home. Like they're doing for Peanut," I say.

"Maybe," Dad says. "But the *Nothosaurus* was surviving just fine in the wild."

Peanut drags behind a little. Sometimes I forget that he's still a baby. I pick him up. I'm tired too, but I can carry him for a little bit. Then it'll be Sam's turn.

"Do you think Peanut should be in the wild?" I ask.

"He's young. He still needs you," Dad says.

Peanut licks my cheek. I think he agrees.

Sightings Are Not Guaranteed

We pitch our tent near the river. We are at the very edge of DECoW land.

"Bart's River Monster Tours is just up the path," Dad says.

"Is that where you saw the *Nothosaurus*?" Sam asks.

"Actually, no. The *Nothosaurus* was a few miles away, near the state park." He points in the other direction.

"Dad, wouldn't a *Nothosaurus* live in salt water?" I ask. "That's what I've read."

"Paleontologists have been wrong before," Dad says. "Our gear is safe here. Let's go find Bart."

I pick up Peanut and shove him in my empty backpack.

"Sorry, little guy." He won't be little much longer. Soon I'll need an extra-large backpack, and then I'll need a tractor trailer.

We hike past trees and more trees and more trees. The only sound comes from the river, the birds, and the dinosaur on my back.

Peanut cries. To cover his sound, Sam sings. I don't know which is more painful.

Dad stops. "There it is."

He points at an old log cabin. A sign nailed to the corner reads *Bart's River Monster Tours.* One motorboat is tied to the dock.

"Try to be quiet, Peanut." I reach into my

backpack and give him a carrot to munch on.

The front door of the cabin is open. We step inside. A man is leaning over a small TV in the corner.

"Hello," Dad says.

"Be with you in a second," the man says without turning around.

I step closer so I can see what's on the TV. It's DECoW! A reporter and about a thousand other people are standing in front of the closed gate.

We all watch and listen.

"There have been no dinosaur sightings," the reporter says. "And the owners are being very quiet. We've been told to expect a press conference in the next day or two."

"Can you believe that?" the man says, still staring at the screen. "The TV people are going nuts over a possible dinosaur sighting. I think I'm going to change the name of my place to Bart's River Dinosaur Tours."

"But you don't have a dinosaur," I say.

"If it'll bring in customers, I'll call it a unicorn." He finally turns around. "I'm Bart."

Dad shakes his hand. "You don't remember me?"

Bart squints hard.

"I'm Brian Mudd," Dad says. "And this is my son, Frank. And my niece Sam."

"Brian Mudd!" Bart exclaims. "I haven't seen you since middle school. You didn't have a beard then, did ya?"

"I didn't." Dad laughs.

Bart nods slowly like he's thinking. "Of course I remember you. You were there the first time I ever saw the river monster. You were the one who scared it off."

"It's not a monster," I say.

"What did you call it again?" Bart asks Dad.

"A *Nothosaurus*," Dad says. "Which is not a dinosaur and certainly not a monster."

"Dinosaurs didn't live in the water. Prehistoric reptiles did," I explain. "Dinosaurs were terrestrial. That means they lived only on land and not in rivers or oceans or lakes. And they didn't fly either. Pterosaurs were flying prehistoric reptiles, not dinosaurs."

"He thinks he's an expert," Sam says.

"I am."

Sam ignores me and asks Bart, "Do you have any pictures of your river dinosaur?"

"It's not a dinosaur," I mumble. Just then

Peanut gives me a karate chop to my back. So I keep quiet.

"Sure do. All along that wall." He points behind us.

Sam and I hurry over. I'm careful not to turn my back. I don't want Bart to see the wiggling in my backpack.

The pictures are terrible. Dad's pencil drawing is much better. Bart's photos are blurry or dark or taken from far, far, far away.

"This looks like a log," Sam says.

"And this looks like an old tire," I add.

"The river monster is fast," Bart says. "Like lightning. Now, can I interest you in a deluxe tour? It includes iced tea and beef jerky."

"A standard tour is fine," Dad says. He takes out his wallet.

Bart taps a sign near the cash register. *River Monster Sightings Not Guaranteed! NO REFUNDS!*

"Understood," Dad says.

Bart makes us put on smelly life jackets. Then we follow him down to the dock. Peanut doesn't get one. He's still stuck in my backpack.

"I don't trust this guy," I whisper to Sam.

"But you trust your dad, right? They saw a *Nothosaurus* once. I bet we see it again." Sam steps into the boat first.

"Are you ready for the ride of your life?" Bart asks.

Only Sam answers. "Yes!"

The *Monster Catcher*

The boat's name is the *Monster Catcher.* It has lots of scratches and dents. Bart promises that all the holes have been patched.

Sam and I sit up front. Dad is in the middle, and Bart works the motor in the back. I unzip my backpack a little and put it on the seat next to me. Peanut has fallen asleep. Baby dinosaurs need lots of rest.

"Keep your eyes open," Bart says. "The river

monster likes to hide in the shadows."

But we don't see anything except bugs and birds and more bugs. I should have packed a fly swatter.

"When's the last time you spotted the river dinosaur?" Sam asks. She smacks a mosquito.

"Just yesterday. He was in that cove up ahead." Bart drives the boat slowly toward the spot. "We have to be real quiet."

I keep my eyes focused on the water. There are no signs of any prehistoric creatures.

"Look!" Bart yells suddenly.

Splash! The sound comes from behind tall weeds.

"I didn't see. Was that the Notho?" Sam asks.

"Sure was," Bart answers.

"Let's go check it out," Sam says. "Before it gets away."

"Can't do that," Bart replies. "It's dangerous to go into the monster's territory."

"Please," I beg. "I really need to see it, not just hear it."

"Surely, you can get a little closer," Dad says. "If we're careful."

"Sorry, folks." Bart turns the boat around. And Sam stands up.

"I demand to see the Notho. I'll jump in if I have to." She plugs her nose like she's about to go off a diving board.

The boat rocks, and my stomach feels mushy.

"You need to sit in the boat!" I yell. "That's a rule." At least I think it's a rule.

Dad reaches for Sam, and the boat rocks even more. All the moving and yelling wakes up Peanut. He pokes his head out of the backpack. I push him back in.

"Don't make me jump!" Sam warns.

"If you get in the river, the monster might eat you," Bart says.

"The *Nothosaurus* is a fish eater," I say, taking

my eyes off of Peanut for a second. "It wouldn't eat a human girl. Probably."

Peanut leaps from the backpack. He lands on Sam's seat.

"Whoa! What in the world is that?" Now Bart is standing up too.

"Nothing!" I grab Peanut and shove him under the seat.

"Everyone sit down." Dad holds out his hands for balance.

"That's *the* dinosaur! The one from DECoW."

Bart's eyes are huge, and I worry that they might fall out of his face.

"It's our ugly cat," Sam says.

"Meow," I say, covering my mouth with my hand.

Bart shakes his head, and then he points a finger in Dad's face. "Wait a second. I remember now. You lived at the dinosaur center."

"No!" I shout. "You're confused. My dad grew up on a cactus ranch."

Bart gives me an angry look.

"Everyone, relax," Dad says. "And please sit down."

Bart wipes his forehead and takes a seat. Then Dad tells him everything, which I think is a really bad idea.

"Now that you know all the Mudd secrets, can you please take us closer to the Notho?" I ask. Peanut crawls out from under the bench and sits in my lap.

"I really can't take you to the monster," Bart says quietly.

"Why?" Dad asks.

"You'll see." Bart drives the boat around the cove to where we heard the noise.

I lean over the edge of the boat, looking for the creature. But instead of seeing a Notho, I see a brick tied to a lever. The contraption has a long rope that sinks into the water. Bart must have pulled the rope and caused the splash.

"You tried to trick us!" I yell.

Sam shakes her head. "I'll never trust any grown-ups again. Never."

"I just . . . ," Bart mumbles. "The river monster . . . it's very shy. I've only seen it a few times."

"What? How do you stay in business?" Sam throws her hands in the air.

"I also offer fishing tours. I always catch a lot of trout. That I promise you." Bart smiles big like he does in his commercials.

"When is the last time you saw the Notho?" Dad asks.

"Almost two years ago," Bart says. "But that might have been a big fish. The best look I ever got was when we were kids."

Dad hangs his head, and his shoulders droop.

I believe Bart is telling the truth *this* time. That means the *Nothosaurus* is probably long gone.

A Seasick Peanut?

Bart drives the boat up and down the river for another hour. There's no sign of the *Nothosaurus*.

"Why are you worried about finding my river dinosaur if you already have a land dinosaur?" Bart asks.

"For science," I answer. "We want to know what prehistoric creatures are still around."

"And Uncle Brian wants to prove that he

really saw a river dinosaur when he was a boy," Sam adds.

"I don't think we're going to prove anything today," Bart says. "It's time we turn this boat around."

The ride back is quiet, until Peanut suddenly gets excited. He jumps onto the edge of the boat and looks into the water below. He whines and makes a clicking noise in his throat. I've heard him do this before. I stare out at the water, hoping to see what Peanut senses.

"Is he okay?" Bart asks.

"Maybe he's seasick," Sam says.

Peanut growls. It's the loudest sound he's ever made.

I reach for him. But before I can grab him, the boat flips over. For a split second, I'm flying through the air. Then I'm in the river.

Water gets in my nose and mouth. I kick to get to the surface. I take a gulp of air.

"Everyone okay?" Dad yells. We're all in the river. We bob up and down, thanks to the life jackets.

"Peanut!" I yell. "Where are you?" He doesn't have a life jacket. And he's only ever been swimming in a baby pool where he can touch the bottom.

"There he is!" Sam yells.

Peanut is crawling out of the water and onto the bank. He must be a good swimmer to have gotten all the way across by himself.

"What happened?" I ask.

The *Monster Catcher* is floating upside down. The river carries it away.

"We must have hit something," Dad says. He swims toward me and Sam.

"Or something hit us," Bart says. "I've been giving tours for ten years, and this has never happened."

"Do you think the *Nothosaurus* flipped the boat?" Sam asks.

"It's the only thing that makes sense," Bart says. "Now I better get my boat before it floats to Montana." Bart swims away.

Sam, Dad, and I dog-paddle toward shore. Peanut is waiting for us in the tall grass.

"Dad, do *you* think it was the *Nothosaurus*?" I ask.

"It would take a big animal to—"

"Whoa!" Sam screams. "Something bumped my leg."

"You're just trying to scare us," I say. At least that's what I hope she's doing.

But then something brushes my leg too. The water is too cloudy and brown to see what it is.

"There's something in the water!" I yell.

"Probably just a fish," Dad says. We all swim faster.

Peanut is running back and forth on the riverbank. He whines and makes the clicking sound in his throat. He did the same thing when we discovered a *Velociraptor* a few weeks ago.

Either he can sense other prehistoric animals, or he's calling to them. I wish he'd be quiet until we get out of the river.

"If it *is* a *Nothosaurus,* it doesn't eat people," I say. "It eats fish." Of course, there weren't people when the Notho was first on the planet. Maybe now it does eat humans.

"Just keep swimming," Dad says. He gives me a little push.

Finally, my feet touch bottom, and I rush out of the river. Sam and Dad are right behind me. We turn around. Bart pulls his boat toward the shore.

"I'd better help him," Dad says.

I pick up a wet Peanut. We stare at the river. I want to see whatever flipped the boat and tickled my leg. Now that I'm safe on land.

"Look!" Sam yells. But it's not a *Nothosaurus* she's pointing to. It's her plastic microphone. She splashes into the water to grab it.

I just shake my head.

Sam smiles as she gets out of the river for a second time.

"This is Sam McCarthy reporting from the river where I was almost eaten alive by a *Nothosaurus,* a prehistoric shark dinosaur." She talks to the invisible camera that she thinks follows her everywhere.

"A *Nothosaurus* is not a shark or a dinosaur," I say, also to the invisible camera.

"Well, whatever it is, we're going to find it," Sam says.

Fishing for the Notho

That night, we build a campfire and hang our clothes to dry. PopPop packed us stuff for s'mores.

Sam gives Peanut a marshmallow.

"He's not supposed to have sugar," I say. "It's not healthy."

"But he really wanted one," Sam says.

I write in my dino journal that Peanut ate a marshmallow. Gram will want to know in case he breaks out in a rash or something. We keep track of everything he eats and what comes out the other end. It's a gross job, but that's science.

"It's getting late," Dad says. "Take Peanut for a quick walk so he can go to the bathroom, and then we'll turn in."

"Okay," I say. I put the leash on Peanut and grab a flashlight. I walk him behind a few trees.

"Go potty," I tell him. He doesn't understand what that means. His English isn't very good.

Peanut pulls on the leash. He runs to the left. He runs to the right. He circles a tree. He digs at a rock.

Snap! It comes from behind us. I shine my flashlight in that direction. There's nothing.

"Hurry up, please," I whisper.

Finally, Peanut goes to the bathroom. Number one. I'll have to write it in the notebook when we get back to the tent. But Peanut isn't ready to go back. He pulls me toward the river.

"No." I tug the leash.

Peanut yanks, and I have to hold really tight. Then he whines and makes the clicking sound in his throat. The hair on my arms stands up.

I grab Peanut and run back to the tent. I stumble over a root but get right back up.

"Frank, what's wrong?" Dad asks.

"There's something . . ." I point back at the trees. But I never saw anything. I only heard a twig snap. That could have been a squirrel or just the wind. I shouldn't make Dad nervous.

"Never mind," I say.

Dad puts out the fire with a bucket of river water. Sam and I clean up all the food. We don't want any animals coming into camp as we sleep. Then we all crawl into the tent. Dad kisses us good night. A minute later, he's snoring.

"Hey," Sam whispers just as I'm falling asleep.

"Go to sleep," I say.

"You saw something when you took Peanut for a walk," she says. "Didn't you?"

"No, I didn't." I would turn over if Peanut weren't on top of me.

"You don't run for no reason, Frank Mudd. What's going on?" Her stinky breath is in my face.

"I swear, I didn't *see* anything," I say. "But Peanut whined like he did on the boat. He knows there's something out there."

"Cool," Sam says. "Let's go find it."

"Okay." I unzip my sleeping bag. Peanut stands and stretches.

"Really?" she asks. "I thought you'd say, 'It's against the rules to explore the river at night.'"

"Now that you put it that way," I say, "it probably isn't a good idea."

"Too late." Sam grabs my arm and drags me out of the tent. Peanut follows us. Dad snores on.

We have a flashlight, and the moon is full. It's pretty easy to see.

"Wait here," Sam says. She walks behind the tent and comes back with a fishing pole and a big net.

"Where did you get those?" I ask.

"I borrowed them from the River Monster shop," Sam answers.

"Does Bart know you borrowed his stuff?" I ask.

"Maybe," Sam says.

Sam and I walk down to the riverbank. Peanut trots along. He's not on a leash. I may have to use the net on *him*.

"A *Nothosaurus* is too big to catch on a fishing pole. It probably weighs more than you and me and Dad all together," I say.

"Whatever." Sam casts the fishing line into the river.

Sam doesn't catch anything on her first try or second or ninth. I sit down on the ground. Peanut climbs into my lap. We're both tired.

"Sam, maybe it's time to give up. I think we need–"

"I got something!" Sam yells. "And it's huge."

Not a Lucky Day

"Help me!" Sam yells.

I grab the fishing pole, and we pull. The rod bends like a rainbow. I worry it might break.

Peanut stands on the edge of the river. He stares at the dark water.

"Don't let go," Sam says.

I hold tight, and Sam reels in the line.

My hands hurt. Could we really have caught a *Nothosaurus*?

Nope. A big fish jumps out of the water. Sam reels in more line. Together we pull the fish to the shore.

"I thought I'd caught a dinosaur," Sam says. The fish flops around on the ground.

"A *Nothosaurus* would break the pole or drag us into the river," I say. "And it's not a dinosaur."

Sam bends down over the fish. Peanut sniffs it.

"Do you think Gram could make him into fish sticks?" she asks, pointing.

"Probably not," I say. "I don't like fish anyway."

Sam carefully pulls the hook out of the fish's mouth.

"It's your lucky day, fish. Back you go," Sam says. She picks it up behind the gills and throws it over the river.

But right before the fish hits the water, a huge mouth pops up and swallows it whole.

"I guess it *wasn't* the fish's lucky day," I say.

Peanut growls at the water.

"Was that the Notho?" Sam asks.

"I didn't get a good look. But I don't know what else it could be," I say.

Sam picks up the fishing pole. "We need to catch more fish and feed our new friend."

I should probably get Dad. But I don't know for sure yet what ate our fish. So I stay with Sam. A few minutes later, she's caught another fish. This one is smaller, and she doesn't need my help.

"Your turn," she says. She gives me the small fish.

Instead of throwing it into the river, I place it right on the edge. The fish flops, trying to get back in the water. Peanut moves closer to it.

"No, buddy," I say. "I don't want you to be mistaken for a snack." I grab Peanut.

The fish makes it into the water. But he's

unlucky too. A large creature swims up behind him and swallows him.

The creature quickly turns back toward the deeper water. But not before I get a look at it. It's the size of a canoe, with a skinny snout and a long neck. The tail is thin, not like a fish or dolphin.

"That was awesome," Sam says. Then she's fishing again.

I keep my eyes on the water, waiting to see the creature. Peanut helps me look.

It takes Sam a bunch of tries to catch the third fish. It's small too. She takes it off the hook and leaves it on the shore.

"We should probably back up," I say.

We take a giant step away from the shore. The fish wiggles in the dirt. Peanut whines and makes his clicking sound. I know what's coming.

The creature crawls out of the river on its four webbed feet. Its big eyes glow in the moonlight. It swallows the fish whole. Then it stares at us.

"Is it a *Nothosaurus*?" Sam whispers.

I nod.

"Is it going to eat us?" she asks.

I shrug.

"I think it's still hungry," Sam says. "I'm going to get more fish."

"Okay," I whisper.

Sam walks farther down the bank and throws the line into the river.

"Let me know if it's going to attack," Sam says.

The *Nothosaurus* isn't ready to attack. It lies down on the shore. It stretches its long neck and rubs its head on the ground. I move closer with my flashlight.

Its skin is dark purple. I notice scars on its front feet and along its back. Most animals that live in the wild have scars because they don't go to the vet for medicine or stitches. Its neck and tail are long and thin. And there's a small fin down the tail. That makes the Notho a good swimmer.

Peanut wiggles to get out of my arms. I set him down. He walks around the *Nothosaurus* but doesn't get too close.

"Got one!" Sam yells.

The Notho lifts its head. A moment later, Sam tosses the fish in our direction. The Notho catches it in midair.

"Hey, girl, did you skip dinner or something?" I ask the Notho. I don't really know if she's a girl. It's a guess.

I give her a small pat on the back. She lets me rub her slimy skin. She feels like a stingray. I petted one once at the aquarium.

I think I've made a new friend, until I hear Dad yell.

"Frank!"

The Notho snaps at my hand but doesn't actually bite me. And then she splashes back into the river.

Doesn't Like Grown-Ups

Peanut splashes into the water after the *Nothosaurus.* I run into the river and grab his tail. Dad follows me and pulls us both out.

"What are you doing?" Dad asks. His face is white.

"We found the *Nothosaurus,*" Sam says proudly. "She likes fish."

"That's not safe. It almost bit off your arm, Frank," Dad says.

"She was just scared," I say.

"She?" Dad says. He scratches his beard. "How did you get her to come out of the water?"

"We fed her a snack," Sam says. "Fresh fish."

"Do you think she would like more?" Dad asks.

"Definitely," Sam says. She catches another fish. Sam's really good at fishing. Not that I'd tell her that.

We put the fish on the shore. And we wait. The *Nothosaurus* doesn't come for her meal. We wait some more. Finally, Sam picks up the fish and drops it into the water. It swims away without getting gobbled up.

"Maybe the Notho is full," I say.

"Or maybe she doesn't like grown-ups," Sam says. "No offense, Uncle Brian."

We go back to our tent. My body is tired, especially my eyes. They don't want to stay open. But my brain is wide-awake. I just met a

Nothosaurus, a prehistoric animal that's been living in the wilds of Wyoming for at least twenty years.

But somehow I fall asleep.

The next thing I know, the sun is up, and someone is yelling good morning.

"What time is it?" I ask.

"Too early," Sam says. She covers her head with a pillow.

I follow Dad out of the tent. Bart waves at us.

"Good morning, campers. I brought you breakfast," Bart says. He holds up a paper bag from the Burger Barn.

Sam flies out of the tent. "Did someone say breakfast?"

Bart laughs. "I got a few breakfast sandwiches. Didn't know what you'd like."

"As long as it's not fish," Sam says. "I'm sick of fish."

"Did you catch fish for dinner?" Bart asks.

"No," Sam says. "We caught fish for the Noth—"

I elbow Sam in her side. "Shh."

"For the river monster?" Bart asks. "You *saw* the monster?"

"No, we caught fish for The Nothing." Sam pushes me forward. "That's what Frank calls his invisible friend. The Nothing."

Bart turns to Dad. "What's going on?" His eyebrows make an angry V.

"The kids may have seen the *Nothosaurus*." Dad shrugs. I don't know why he keeps telling Bart all our secrets.

"Really? You kids just lured it in with fresh fish?" Bart asks. I expected him to be angry. He's not.

"Well, I did most of the fishing," Sam says. "The Notho likes me."

"This is great." Bart claps his hands together. "Then you can help me catch it."

"What? No!" I say, and look to Dad for help.

"No one is going to catch the *Nothosaurus,*" Dad says. "She doesn't belong to anyone. She's a wild animal."

Peanut steps out of the tent. He stretches and yawns.

"And *that's* not a wild animal?" Bart points at Peanut.

I jump in front of him. Peanut is not wild. And he's mine.

"He's only a baby. He can't live in the wild."
Sam puts her hands on her hips.

"We don't want to cause any trouble," Dad says.

"Are those my fishing poles?" Bart asks. He
spots the gear we used last night.

"We needed to borrow them," Sam explains.

"Sam," Dad says. "You took those without
asking?"

She shrugs and gives him a big smile. "I was
going to bring them back."

"We didn't think anyone would mind," I say.
Not that taking the poles was my idea.

"I think it's time you went home," Bart says.

"This is DECoW property," I say. "We *are*
home."

"Just stay away from my river and my monster," Bart growls.

It's not his river and it's not his monster, but
I don't correct him. Grown-ups don't like to be
corrected by kids. Maybe they don't like to be

corrected by other grown-ups either. I don't know for sure.

"We won't bother you again," Dad says. "Sorry for any trouble." Dad hands Bart the fishing gear.

"Thanks for breakfast," Sam says as Bart walks away.

"No worries," Bart says. "I know exactly how you're going to repay me."

Bring Out the Dinosaur

Sam and I sit on the edge of the river. I wish we were leaving today, but we need to give Gram and PopPop more time to get things ready at DECoW.

It's too hot to do anything but dip our feet in the water. Peanut munches on the low branches of a cottonwood tree.

"I'm bored," Sam says. We both want to see

the *Nothosaurus* again. I use the binoculars to scan the river. Without fish, the Notho probably won't stop by for lunch.

I give Sam a turn with the binoculars.

"Uh-oh," she says a minute later. "Someone's coming."

I take the binoculars and look. The *Monster Catcher* motors up the river. Bart is not alone. Every seat in the boat is taken. Six people with cameras are coming our way.

"Good thing the *Nothosaurus* isn't here," Sam says.

I nod. But then a thought hits my brain.

"They're not here for the *Nothosaurus*. They came to see Peanut." I grab my dinosaur and dive into the tent. Sam is right behind me. Dad joins us and zips the tent closed.

"Can we go back to Gram and PopPop's house now?" I ask.

"There will be even more people at DECoW,"

Dad reminds me. "The whole world wants to meet Peanut."

"We can't stay here," I say.

Bart calls to us with his megaphone. "Frank Mudd, bring out the dinosaur. The people want to see him."

We wait inside the tent for ten minutes. Bart and his visitors stay in the boat and keep calling for the dinosaur.

Peanut stares at me like I should know what to do. I shrug because I don't have a good plan.

"They're not leaving," I say.

"I'll talk to them," Sam says. "I'm almost famous. I'm used to dealing with fans."

"You were in a commercial like a hundred years ago," I shoot back.

Sam doesn't reply. Instead, she slips out of the tent.

"Ladies and gentlemen," I hear Sam say, "who would like an autograph?"

"Oh boy," Dad says. "I'd better take care of this."

Dad crawls out of the tent. But before he gets it closed, Peanut darts through the small opening. I grab for him and miss.

"Noooo!" I yell. The zipper gets stuck, and I can't get out. I pull. I yank. I twist. Finally, I tumble out into the dirt. Dad helps me up.

Sam is holding Peanut. They're only a few feet from the water. Everyone in the boat is taking pictures except for a teenager.

"It's not a real dinosaur!" the teenager shouts. Then he pulls out an apple and throws it at Peanut.

Thwump! The apple hits Peanut on his horn.

Peanut cries out and leaps from Sam's arms. I run toward him. But something beats me there.

The *Nothosaurus* glides out of the river. She stares at Peanut with her head high in the air.

She growls at the people. It's a warning.

No one talks or moves. The Notho sniffs Peanut. She taps his head with her webbed foot. I think she wants to make sure he's okay.

Peanut rubs his horn against her snout.

It feels like an hour before Peanut leaves the *Nothosaurus*'s side. He runs over to me, and I pick him up. He smells a bit fishy.

The Notho looks at me and then turns to the boat. She gives an angry growl before slipping back into the water.

The people on the boat all start talking at once. Everyone except for Bart, that is. His mouth hangs open, and his eyes are wide.

"That was incredible," Dad says.

"Meh." Sam shrugs. "You've seen one prehistoric creature, you've seen them all." I know Sam is joking. At least she better be.

"Are you okay, Bart?" Dad calls out.

Bart snaps out of his trance and finally blinks. "Stay here," he tells his passengers. Then he steps out of the boat into the knee-high water and wades over to Dad.

"Well?" Dad says.

"It's more amazing than I remembered," Bart

says. "What a beautiful animal. I've never seen her out of the water or for so long. Wow."

"You aren't going to try to catch her, are you?" Sam asks.

"No. Not at all." Bart smiles. Maybe he needed to see the *Nothosaurus* even more than we did.

"Hey!" the teenager yells from the boat. "I want to hold the dinosaur. I want a selfie with that thing."

"No," Bart says before I can. "You are officially banned from Bart's *Nothosaurus* Tours forever. And no refund."

Bart goes back to his boat and starts the motor. We wave goodbye and watch them disappear down the river.

"Do you think Bart will be back with more customers?" I ask.

"I don't know," Dad says. "But let's move our camp away from the river just in case. Peanut's had enough visitors for one day."

First Time for Everything

"**W**hy didn't we bring the truck?" I ask. We've been walking for only five minutes, and I'm beat. Somehow our camping stuff weighs even more than it did yesterday.

"You can't drive a truck out here," Dad says.

"Duh, there are no roads," Sam adds.

"Then we should have taken a helicopter or something," I say.

Every part of me is sweaty, even under my

fingernails and in my ears. Maybe that's why I think I hear an engine. I look back at the river, and then at the sky. No boats. No helicopters.

"Could a bus drive out here? Because I think I hear a bus." I hope Dad has money for a ticket back to DECoW.

Sam rolls her eyes.

"Look!" I point toward the east. Or maybe it's the west. A dust cloud trails a skinny vehicle. I pick up Peanut.

"That's Aaron," Sam says.

It's a four-wheeler. And maybe our ride home.

"And there's someone else behind him," Sam says.

I squint to see better. Dad waves his arms above his head.

Aaron comes to a stop in front of us. He flips back his helmet.

"Hey," Aaron says. "We've been looking for you."

Then the second four-wheeler pulls up. The driver takes off the dark helmet.

"Gram?" I yell.

"Cool," Sam says. "I didn't know you rode four-wheelers!"

"There's a first time for everything." Gram jumps off.

"Can you give us a ride back?" I ask. "My feet are ready to fall off."

"You can't come back yet," Gram says. "DECoW is crazy right now. People are lined up at the gate, and we aren't even open."

"We can't stay here," I say.

Sam jumps excitedly. "The river is full of crazy stuff like a *Nothosaurus* and a man named Bart who thinks Peanut is a tourist attraction."

"*Nothosaurus?*" Aaron asks. "You found another dinosaur without me?" He throws his helmet on the ground.

"It's not a dinosaur," I correct. "It's a prehistoric reptile."

"Close enough. We said the next dinosaur we found was mine. So this *thing* is mine." Aaron crosses his arms.

"Well, you've got to catch her first," Sam says.

"No one is catching the Notho," Dad says. "She lives in the wild."

"You saw it?" Gram asks.

Dad nods and explains the whole story. He tells her about Bart and how the Notho likes fish but not grown-ups.

"She's been out here all these years," Gram says. "That's impressive."

I look at Gram. "Do you think Peanut would be happier in the wild?"

"No, Frank." Gram smiles. "When Peanut is fully grown, he will be bigger than a barn. The world has changed a lot in sixty-five million years. He's going to need us to take care of him and keep him safe."

Peanut digs a hole in the dirt. It's hard to imagine him being bigger than me someday.

"When can we go back to DECoW?" Sam asks.

"In two more days," Gram says. "The builders are marking the location of Peanut's habitat. We want to show the public where he'll be living."

"People are scared. They think we're going

to let a dinosaur run around and eat people," Aaron says. "But he's an herbivore. He eats broccoli, not humans."

Peanut won't eat anyone, but he may accidentally stomp on someone if he gets as big as we think he will.

Gram and Aaron help us move our camp farther away from the river. And Gram gives us the extra supplies she brought.

"Aaron, do you want to stay?" Dad asks. "We can squeeze one more sleeping bag in the tent."

"No thanks," Aaron says. "The junior fishing tournament starts at sunrise. I need to be ready."

"Sam, you should enter the tournament," I say. "You caught a bunch of fish last night."

"I'm a really good fisherman. It wouldn't be fair to the other kids," Sam says. "But you could enter, Frank."

"Haha," I say. I know when I'm being made fun of.

Goldie

For the rest of the day and that night, we don't see Bart or the *Nothosaurus*. The next morning, I spend some time writing in my notebook. I don't want to forget anything about the Notho.

Species: *Nothosaurus*
Size: as long as two of me
Color: grayish-purple

Features: thin snout, sharp teeth, black eyes,
    four webbed feet, long neck, and long,
    skinny tail with a fin
Food: fish
Name: ?

Sam is reading over my shoulder. She taps the name spot.

"Name her Goldie," she says.

"But she's not gold," I say.

"I want to name her after my favorite pet," Sam says.

"You don't have any pets," I say.

"I won a goldfish at the fair, and her name was Goldie. She was a good fish. She lived with us for almost a whole week."

I write down Goldie. I can always change it.

We eat granola bars and bananas for breakfast. I share my banana with Peanut. He's about to take a bite, but then stops. He lifts his head.

I know he hears something.

I stand up. It takes a second, but I hear it too. Someone is yelling.

"Brian! Frank! Sam!"

"Bart is coming this way," I say. "Run!"

"I'm not running," Sam says. "It's too hot."

It's not too hot for Bart to run. He jogs across the field.

"What's wrong?" Dad asks Bart.

Bart bends over and takes three big breaths.

"The *Nothosaurus,*" he says. "It's attacking the fishing tournament."

"What?" Sam yells. "Goldie wouldn't attack anything or anyone."

"They're trying to catch it," Bart says.

"Who?" Dad asks.

"Everyone. The police, firefighters, ranchers. They might hurt her." Bart looks at me and Sam. "Maybe you could help her. She likes you. She trusts you."

"Yeah, we can," Sam says. "Let's go."

I turn to grab Peanut, but he's already crawled into my backpack.

"Good dino," I say.

We run across the field toward the river. It's easier without all the gear on our backs. Bart's boat is tied up. We jump on board and put on our life jackets.

"Hang on." Bart revs the boat's engine. We race down the river.

"How far?" I scream my question because the motor is so loud. But Bart doesn't need to answer. Just up ahead, I can see hundreds of people on the riverbanks.

Bart ties the boat to a dock.

"I'm going to find out what's happening," Dad says. He hops out of the boat and walks up to a fireman.

"There's Aaron." I spot him standing in the river. The water only comes up to his knees. He's waving his arms, trying to get everyone to calm down.

"Come on!" Sam jumps out. I follow her with Peanut in the backpack. We splash our way to Aaron.

"Have you seen the *Nothosaurus*?" I ask.

"Yeah! It's huge," Aaron says. "I think we should call him Big Daddy."

"*She's* already got a name," Sam says. "It's Goldie."

"Goldie?" Aaron asks.

I grab both Aaron's and Sam's sleeves. "Not now! Aaron, tell us what happened."

"Well, I was winning the tournament. I had eight fish in the first hour. One was at least twenty inches. And—"

Sam cuts in. "Tell us about the *Nothosaurus*."

"I was pulling in fish number nine when something bit it right off my line," Aaron says. "I thought maybe I just lost the fish. But I never let 'em get away."

"Never?" Sam asks.

"Hardly ever," Aaron says. "So I was tying on a new lure when I heard kids screaming. The *Nothosaurus* is a fish thief. It took fish off the lines. It took fish off the shore. It took fish from a cooler."

"Well, you are kind of taking *her* fish," I say. "She lives out here. She needs to eat."

"And we may have accidentally taught her

that kids will feed her fish," Sam says with a shrug.

"Where is she now?" I look around the river. All I see is people. People walking in the water. People riding in boats.

"They have her cornered in that cove," Aaron says.

"What are they going to do to her?" Sam asks.

The grown-ups have nets and giant hooks and other tools that could hurt Goldie.

"We'd better do something," I say.

"What?" Sam asks.

"I've always wanted to ride a real live dinosaur," Aaron says.

Riding a Dino

"**Y**ou're not riding Goldie," I say. "And she's not a dinosaur. But you've given me an idea. We need to show them that the *Nothosaurus* is friendly. Do you have any more fish?"

"Still got eight. The tournament hasn't been canceled yet." He points to his blue cooler on shore.

"We need them," I say.

"Can I at least keep the big one?" he asks.

Sam pulls him by the collar of his shirt. "Come on."

Aaron grabs his cooler of fish. Then we run to Bart's boat. After we explain, he has us across the river in no time. Aaron, Sam, and I jump out.

I know the *Nothosaurus* is friendly. But she still might attack the people trying to catch her.

"Oh no, look," Sam says. A news van is parked on the side of the road. No matter what happens, we will be on TV.

We run toward the far end of the cove.

"Stop!" a policeman yells. "There's a dangerous animal in these waters."

"Pretend you don't hear him," Sam says.

We get to the tip of the cove. Aaron puts down the cooler. I gently drop my backpack. Sam pulls out a dead fish.

"Here, Goldie," she calls in a sweet voice. "Come on, Goldie. We have fish for you."

Peanut jumps and growls inside the backpack.

He almost rolls himself into the river.

"Sorry, buddy. Just hang in there for a little while longer." I pick up the bag and move it farther from the edge.

Sam holds the fish over the water. There's no sign of the Notho.

"Throw it into the water," Aaron says.

Sam tosses the dead fish. It floats down the river like a raft. The Notho doesn't take the bait.

"We don't want to hurt you." Sam pulls another fish out of the cooler.

"Hey, how many are you going to take?" Aaron asks.

"As many as we need," Sam snaps back.

Sam throws a second fish into the water. And then a third. And then a fourth.

"No more." Aaron slams the cooler closed.

"Yes more," Sam says in his face.

"We have to try something else," I say.

Peanut flips over in his backpack again. I unzip it just a little. I rub his horn.

"Not much longer," I tell him. "We are trying to rescue a not-a-dinosaur."

Peanut gives me his big, sad eyes. That's when I realize that every time we've seen the *Nothosaurus,* it's Peanut who has been waiting for her on the shore.

"Goldie likes Peanut!" I shout.

"You're not going to throw Peanut in the river, are you?" Aaron asks.

"No way," I answer. "But Peanut can call Goldie. It's like they have a special code."

I start to unzip the backpack.

Sam puts her hand on my arm. "If you take him out, everyone will see. The secret won't be a secret."

"It'll be the opposite of a secret," Aaron says.

More boats join the hunt for the *Nothosaurus*. One has a big harpoon on board.

"We have to save Goldie," I say. "And I know Peanut wants to help too."

"Okay," Sam says. "Do it."

I take Peanut out of the backpack. He's so happy, he looks like he's smiling. I put him down on the edge of the river.

"Do your thing," I say.

Peanut looks at the water, and then he whines in his strange dinosaur voice and makes the clicking noise.

People look in our direction. They point. Some scream.

"I hope this works," Sam says.

"Just get another fish," I say.

Both Aaron and Sam hold a fish over the water. Peanut keeps calling for our new friend.

"Please, Goldie," I whisper. "We want to help you."

Out of the corner of my eye, I see two policemen coming our way.

"Hey, what are you doing?" one yells.

My legs shake because I want to grab Peanut and run. And I'm about to when Goldie jumps out of the water and onto the shore.

Sam claps with excitement. Aaron falls back on his butt. Peanut runs over to the *Nothosaurus.* He puts his horn to her snout.

"Goldie!" Sam yells. She throws a fish, and Goldie catches it in her mouth. She swallows it in one gulp.

"Want another?" Aaron asks, and throws his fish.

"Step back!" a policeman demands.

People get closer and closer. I run in front of Goldie.

"This is a *Nothosaurus*!" I yell to the crowd,

including the TV camera. "She's a prehistoric reptile."

Sam whips out her plastic microphone. "Yes, she's a prehistoric reptile and not a dinosaur. Got it?"

Aaron moves closer to the *Nothosaurus* on the other side. We've got her well protected from nets and hooks and anything else.

"She eats fish. And she's not going to hurt anyone. She's been living in Wyoming for over twenty years." I point at my dad, who is standing on the other side of the river. "My dad saw the *Nothosaurus* when he was a boy. She likes it here."

"Step away from the animal," a man says. He's carrying a hook with a big rope attached.

"Just let her go back in the water," I say. "She's a good girl."

"Move away," the man says again.

"Never!" Aaron yells. Then, suddenly, he

jumps on Goldie's back like she's a horse. "Giddyup."

Goldie dives back into the river. Aaron stays on her back. Well, for a little while, at least. Goldie goes under the water, and Aaron floats to the top. The boats move out of the way, and the *Nothosaurus* swims down the river.

"That was awesome!" Aaron yells. "I rode a dinosaur. First human ever to ride a dinosaur."

"She's not a dinosaur!" Sam says to Aaron.

Then she turns to the news camera. "You got that. The *Nothosaurus* is *not* a dinosaur."

The news lady nods her head. "Got it. The animal in the river is not a dinosaur." Then she points behind me at Peanut. "But that certainly is."

Do Not Feed the *Nothosaurus*

Two days later, we finally invite all the TV cameras to DECoW to officially meet Peanut and to hear about his new home. I'm nervous and excited. And I'm pretty sure I'm going to throw up.

Dad didn't let the reporter ask us any questions at the river. She sure tried.

Where did the dinosaur come from?

What type of dinosaur is it?

What does it eat?

Are there more?

Everything is set up in the DECoW parking lot. Gram stands behind the microphones with PopPop, Sam, and Dad at her side. Aaron and his parents are in the front row. I wait inside DECoW. My job is to bring Peanut out at the end.

Saurus stays with me and Peanut. She's like our bodyguard or attack cat.

Through the door, I can hear Gram giving the reporters all the details about Peanut. I read her speech last night to make sure she got it all right.

Peanut's new home still isn't built. Gram and the Crabtrees put up a fence for now. But we will have to build a wall and maybe a moat to keep a full-size Peanut in and to keep visitors out.

"It's hard to imagine you so big," I say to him. He puts his horn to my nose.

Finally, PopPop opens the door. "Frank, it's time."

Saurus leads the way. I walk out and stand next to Gram.

"Ladies and gentlemen," Gram says, "I give you Peanut, the world's only living *Wyomingasaurus*."

My stomach flips, and my knees shake. But Peanut seems happy. I hold him high so that everyone can see him. Peanut lifts his head and smiles. Sort of.

Gram answers questions from the crowd. She shows them a map and pictures of Peanut's new home. The questions don't end until Peanut starts squirming and tries to get away from me.

"It's okay, Peanut. We're almost done," I whisper in his ear.

But Peanut keeps twisting and even nips at my fingers.

The crowd gasps.

"Peanut, stop." I hug him tight to my chest.

"What's going on?" Sam asks. "Why is he upset?"

"I don't know." Then, suddenly, I do. A warm liquid soaks my shirt.

Aaron starts laughing. "Frank is covered in Peanut pee."

· · ·

That night, we order pizza for dinner, and PopPop makes us root beer floats. We turn off the TV and the computer. We know the whole world is talking about Peanut. But we are all Peanut experts here.

"Mom says she's coming next weekend," Dad says. "She can't wait to meet Peanut."

"And my mom will be here soon too," Sam says.

I give Sam a small smile. We have a plan to get our parents to move to Wyoming. It's not really a plan, just a lot of begging. There's no way Saurus and I are leaving Peanut. No one can take care of him like we can.

DECoW will open again in the morning for the first time in four days. But to keep things under control, people need to buy tickets online. We don't want a million visitors at once. Our restrooms aren't big enough. Only two hundred tickets will be sold each day. And there is no guarantee that visitors will get to see Peanut. He's not on display. Not yet anyway.

Goldie has been spotted a bunch of times since the fishing tournament. She's less shy now. The town has put signs along the river: *Do Not Feed the Nothosaurus.* Sam and I broke that rule before it was a rule.

I munch on my pepperoni pizza. Peanut gets a slice of mushroom while Saurus purrs in my lap.

"Do you think things will get back to normal around here?" I ask Gram.

"Not at all!" She laughs. "It's going to be a new normal."

I don't like the sound of that.

"It will be okay," PopPop says. "Peanut is family. As long as we stick together, I'm not worried." But PopPop never worries.

I scoop Peanut up from the floor. He puts his horn to my nose.

"You might not be my secret anymore, but you'll always be my best friend."

At that, Saurus meows.

"One of my best friends." I squeeze them both tight. Having a dinosaur (and a fluffy cat) is still awesome. Even if the whole world knows about it.

Dear Reader,

I guess you can tell everyone about Peanut now. (They probably already know.) I release you from your oath. That means you won't grow gills on your forehead and webbed toes. I think.

Thank you. And if you ever find a real live dinosaur, tell ONLY me. I promise to keep your secret.

Sincerely,
Frank Mudd

Glossary

Here are some words and definitions, in case you aren't a dinosaur expert like me.

dinosaur: A type of prehistoric reptile that lived on land and did not fly. Meat-eaters walked on two legs. Plant-eaters walked on two or four legs. (Talk to your local paleontologist for more info.)

extinct: Wiped out as a species. Plants and animals can go extinct. Like the *Nothosaurus*. Or is it?

herbivore: An animal that eats only salad— I mean, plants.

mammal: A class of animals that are warm-blooded and have fur (or hair). Most mammals are also born alive from a mom, not from an egg.

You are a mammal. (Assuming you are a person and not a bearded dragon.)

Nothosaurus: Not a dinosaur! (See **dinosaur.**) It is a prehistoric reptile that lived in water but could visit land.

paleontologist: A scientist who studies fossils (like dinosaur fossils) to learn about life on Earth long ago.

prehistoric: Before humans began writing things down. Dinosaurs came *way* before humans and *way* before writing.

pterosaurs: Not dinosaurs! (See **dinosaur.**) They are flying prehistoric reptiles.

reptile: In modern times, a group of animals that have scales and are cold-blooded, like alligators and snakes. But in prehistoric times, reptiles also had feathers and could have been warm-blooded. (Talk to your local biologist for more information.)

terrestrial: Refers to animals that live on the ground and not in water or in trees or in the air. Dinos are terrestrial. Humans too!

Velociraptor: A turkey-sized dinosaur that had feathers, ran fast, and ate meat. *Velociraptor* means "speedy thief."

Wyomingasaurus: A dinosaur! This is Peanut's species. The name isn't official yet.

About the Author

Stacy McAnulty does not have a dinosaur. She does have three kids, two dogs, and one husband. She has been on a dinosaur dig in Wyoming, where she found a small fossil. It wasn't an egg. Stacy grew up in upstate New York but now calls North Carolina home. (She still really wants a dinosaur—maybe a *Deinonychus*.) Learn more about The Dino Files at thedinofiles.com.

About the Illustrator

Mike Boldt loves ice cream, comics, and drawing. He is the illustrator of *I Don't Want to Be a Frog* and *I Don't Want to Be Big* and the author and illustrator of *A Tiger Tail*. Mike lives in Alberta, Canada, only a couple of hours from Drumheller, the site of that country's largest collection of dinosaur fossils.

New friends. New adventures.
Find a new series...just for you!

BALLPARK *Mysteries*

FOR THE SPORTS FAN

The DINO Files

FOR THE ADVENTURER

Louise Trapeze

FOR THE SUPERSTAR

PIPER GREEN

FOR THE DREAMER

PUPPY PIRATES

FOR THE ANIMAL LOVER

Totally True adventures!

FOR THE EXPLORER

RandomHouseKids.com

It's a president, it's a cat, it's a plane, it's ... a whole lot of adventure!

Read about mice who live in the White House:

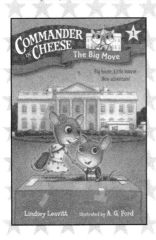

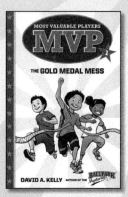
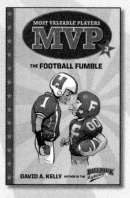